Planning for Murder

Planning for Murder

North Dakota Library Mysteries
Prequel

ELLEN JACOBSON

Planning for Murder

Digital ISBN: 978-1-951495-40-4
Print ISBN: 978-1-951495-41-1
Large Print ISBN: 978-1-951495-42-8

Editor: Lisa Lee Proofreading & Editing

Cover: Molly Burton, Cozy Cover Designs

This novella was originally published as part of the Mysteries, Midsummer Sun and Murders cozy mystery anthology.

First Printing: September 2022

Published by: Ellen Jacobson
www.ellenjacobsonauthor.com

For my library and book-loving sister and
my North Dakotan husband.

CONTENTS

CHAPTER 1
STRAWBERRY SHAMPOO

In my twenty-eight years on this planet, there's one question I never thought I'd have to ask myself —"What do you do if a buffalo tries to lick you to death?"

I know what you're thinking. "Thea, what in the world were you doing getting so close to a buffalo? Don't you know how dangerous that is?"

Believe me, I know you're supposed to keep your distance. My grandparents drilled that into my head on camping trips at Theodore Roosevelt National Park.

"They're dangerous animals. If one of them stops what it's doing and starts paying attention to you, slowly back away," Grandma would say to my brother and me. Then, being the librarian that she is, she'd recommend a few books about buffalo for us to read.

By the way, you can find books about buffalo cataloged under 599.64 at your local library. Quizzes on the Dewey Decimal system were Grandma's idea of fun during road trips when I was a kid, so classifying books comes second nature to me.

"Why didn't you take your grandmother's advice and slowly back away from the buffalo?" some of you are probably wondering.

Well, that's an excellent question. Trust me, if I had seen him coming, I would have gotten the heck out of there.

But that's not what happened. This particular buffalo was very sneaky . . . actually, hang on a minute. I'm getting ahead of myself. Let me rewind and tell you the story from the beginning. I promise we'll get back to the buffalo attack.

It all started the previous night when I discovered someone who I trusted had betrayed me in the worst possible way. Instead of standing my ground and putting up a fight, I took the easy way out and ran away from home.

The last time I had done anything like that, I was eight years old. I shoved my teddy bear and a book into my backpack, left a note on the kitchen table, and then got on my bike and pedaled as fast as I could. I made it all the way to the ice cream parlor before anyone noticed I was missing.

When you're twenty-eight, running away is

different. I used a ballpoint pen instead of crayons to write a note. I got out of town in my fuel-efficient hatchback, not on a pink bike with tassels on the handlebars. And the home I left wasn't a cozy farmhouse in North Dakota that I shared with my brother and grandparents. It was a sleek, modern condo in Minneapolis with spectacular river views.

After ten hours of non-stop driving from Minnesota to western North Dakota, I was exhausted mentally and physically.

Doubts crept in as I neared my destination. What kind of adult runs away from her problems straight back to her childhood home? I thought about heading back to Minneapolis, but then I saw a familiar sign —"Welcome to Why, North Dakota. Why Not Stay a While?" All the tension in my shoulders melted away. Maybe staying a while with family was exactly what I needed.

As I got closer to the sign, I laughed out loud. Someone had spray painted over Why's population number at the bottom of the sign and written "None of Your Business" over it. My money was on Bobby Jorgenson being the culprit. Since leaving school, he had graduated from pulling hair and throwing spitballs to petty theft and vandalism.

I glanced at the clock on the dashboard. It was a little after eleven. My grandparents were creatures of habit—they had lunch at Swede's Norwegian Diner every Monday. Since I hadn't called them to let them know I was coming, I guess I'd surprise them there.

After turning onto the road which led into town, I slowed down right before the speed trap I knew was waiting around the bend. I gave the police officer a jaunty wave, then parked near the town square.

As I got out of the car, I breathed in the scent of freshly mowed grass, smiling at the Fourth of July banners strung around the bandstand. People came from all over for Why's Fourth of July celebration. My timing couldn't be better. I could lick my wounds during the week, then enjoy the parade, picnic, and fireworks on Saturday. After that, I'd head back to my real life in Minneapolis.

I was stretching my arms over my head when I felt something wet pressing against the back of my neck. I froze in place. Whoever it was behind me made low, rumbling noises, and their breath stank.

Thinking it was Bobby Jorgenson up to his old tricks again, I spun around, ready to give him what for. But when I saw what was really behind me, my heart started racing. I was standing face-to-face with a massive buffalo who easily weighed 2,000 pounds and had to have been at least six feet tall at his shoulders.

The buffalo stared at me for a moment, then he licked my face with his smooth tongue. That's when I fainted. Maybe I should have screamed or fought back, but honestly, fainting seemed like a perfectly reasonable reaction. If you're going to be licked to death by a buffalo, do you really want to be awake when it happens?

Eventually I came to, but things only got worse from there. Are you wondering if anything could possibly be worse than death? Believe me, there is.

* * *

As I came to, for a moment, I wasn't sure where I was. Feeling groggy, I sat up and rubbed my eyes. Then I saw the buffalo, and it all came back to me. My body trembled as adrenaline flooded through my system. Was I going to be able to get out of this situation?

The enormous creature stood less than a foot away from me, placidly chewing on something. I inched back toward my car and frantically tried to open the door, but it was locked. My purse was too far away to grab the car keys out of it. I thought about making a run for it, but the buffalo had me trapped.

He pawed the ground with one of his hooves and steam came out of his nostrils as he snorted. This was not a good sign. Any minute now, he was going to charge and trample me. The only thing I could think to do was play dead. I was all set to slump back onto the ground when I noticed something peculiar hanging from the buffalo's mouth—some sort of hair.

I reached up and felt my head. Realizing it was damp, I shuddered. If you've never been covered in buffalo saliva, I don't recommend it. As I ran my hands through my hair, my fingers grazed a tender section at the back of my head. Then I felt a small bald patch. I leaned forward and stared at the hair the buffalo was chewing on. It was long and blond, just like mine.

It's one thing for a buffalo to lick you, but for him to pull a chunk of your hair out for a snack, well, that's the final straw.

I got to my feet, squared my shoulders, then glared at the buffalo. "How dare you?"

His eyes seemed to widen slightly, then he shuffled back a few feet. Surprised by my effect on him, I wondered if I was some sort of buffalo whisperer. I took a step forward. "It's rude to eat people's hair, don't you think?"

He stopped chewing, then lowered his head as if he was ashamed of himself. This was amazing. I could control this massive creature. I waved my hand at him. "Go on, get out of here. Go find your herd."

His response was to snort loudly. Chunks of grass went flying as he pawed the ground. My stomach twisted in knots. He was going to attack. I made a run for it across the town square, my legs pumping as hard as they could. The ground vibrated as the buffalo pursued me.

I could see Swede's diner in the distance. If I could just make it there, I'd be safe. After what seemed like an eternity, I reached the diner and yanked the door open. Once inside, I slammed the door shut.

The buffalo skidded to a stop, then pressed his nose against the glass. I quickly turned the deadbolt. My legs felt like jelly and my breathing was ragged. Not surprising, considering I had narrowly escaped being trampled to death or, worse, being eaten alive.

The buffalo stared at me through the glass. His dark brown eyes were expressive. Curious, even. He'd already sampled my hair. He was probably wondering what the rest of me would taste like.

I chewed my lip. All that stood between me and him was a door. How strong was this glass, anyway? Could it withstand a buffalo charging it? Without thinking, I grabbed a nearby table and positioned it in front of the door as a barricade.

Then something filtered through my consciousness. It was laughter. I shook my head. Who would be laughing at a time like this? Spinning around, I saw Norma Gottlieb, a tall red-head who had been a waitress at the diner for as long as I could remember. She was leaning against the counter, a huge grin plastered across her face.

"Thea Olson," she said. "What in the world are you doing?"

"Bu . . . Bu . . . Buffalo," I spluttered, pointing behind me. "He attacked me."

Norma chuckled. "Ferdinand wouldn't hurt a flea."

"His name's not Ferdinand," a man called out from the kitchen.

"Don't listen to him," Norma said. "He's called Ferdinand."

"His name is Elmer," the man called out again. "Don't make me fire you."

"Is that Swede?" I asked Norma.

"Yep. Grumpy as ever." She turned to the kitchen, cupped her hand to her mouth and yelled, "It's Ferdinand."

I glanced back at the door. The buffalo was still standing there. Surely, the glass would shatter if he even as much as leaned against it.

"Are you and Swede really arguing about what this creature's name is?" I asked. "Shouldn't you be more worried about him getting in here?"

Norma smiled. "We only let him in on special occasions."

I ran my fingers through my hair, cringing as I felt my bald spot. "Have you both lost your minds? That's a wild, dangerous creature out there. He ate my hair."

"Did you use a strawberry-scented shampoo by any chance?" Norma asked. "Ferdinand loves strawberries."

Swede Hanson came out of the kitchen and glared at Norma. The older man hadn't changed a bit since I had last seen him—still short, squat, and bald.

"It's Elmer," he said to the waitress before turning and handing me a bag of carrots. "Feed him some of these. That'll keep him from eating your hair."

Norma dragged the table back to its original

position, then opened the door. The buffalo inched forward, but Norma shooed him away. "You need to get out of the way, Ferdinand. The lunch crowd will be here any minute."

The buffalo obeyed her, going to stand at the edge of the sidewalk. Norma nudged me out the door. "Go on, give Ferdinand his carrots."

My eyes widened as I stood face-to-face with the buffalo. I turned around to protest, but before I could say anything, Norma asked, "Do your grandparents know you're in town?"

"Uh, no. It was an impromptu trip."

"Good timing," Norma said. "I know your grandma is worried about your cousin, Freya. Maybe you can help."

"What's happened to Freya?" I asked, but Norma had already closed the door. I looked back at the buffalo, who was patiently waiting for his snack. My stomach twisted in knots. I wasn't sure what I was more worried about—feeding carrots to a buffalo or what was going on with my cousin.

***

As I was warily feeding the buffalo his last carrot, I saw my grandparents walking toward the diner. They both did a double-take. Grandma rushed up and pulled me into a hug. She was wearing her trademark lavender perfume—a scent I will forever equate with comfort and love.

Grandpa patted my shoulder awkwardly. A stoic individual by nature, he was a man of few words, but the twinkle in his blue eyes told me all I needed to know.

"Thea, what a lovely surprise," Grandma said as she pulled back. "What are you doing here?"

"Do I need an excuse to visit my grandparents?" I asked.

"No, of course not," she said as she adjusted the floral silk scarf around her neck. "But you've been so busy with your job—"

Not wanting to tell my grandparents what had happened with work, I interrupted. "What kind of gelatin salad are you making for the Fourth of July picnic?"

Grandma gave me a knowing look. Well aware that I was trying to change the subject, she went along with it. "I'm not sure yet. Your brother wants that marshmallow pecan one, but there's a new recipe I want to try."

My grandfather cleared his throat and nodded at the diner.

"You go on ahead and grab us a table, Thor," Grandma said to him. "Thea and I will be along in a minute."

After he left, Grandma turned to me. "What's really going on?"

"Nothing," I said. "I just needed to get away from

Minneapolis for a while."

Grandma gave me a gentle smile as my eyes welled up with tears. "You let me know when you're ready to talk, dear." When the buffalo nudged my hand, hoping to find another carrot, Grandma chuckled. "I see you've met Hagrid."

"How many names does this guy have?"

"A lot," she said. "No one can seem to agree on what he should be called."

"Where did he come from?"

"It's a mystery. He showed up here a few months ago. He's a real sweetie." She scratched the buffalo behind his ears for a moment, then said to me, "Come on, we better go join your grandpa."

As we walked toward the diner, I asked about Freya. "Norma said that you're worried about her."

Grandma pursed her lips. "Norma should spend a little less time eavesdropping on private conversations."

"What's going on with Freya?" I prompted.

"I'm afraid your cousin has gotten herself in over her head with her new business venture." Grandma looked around to make sure no one could overhear us, then lowered her voice. "You know all the money she and Josh had been saving for a down payment on a house? Well, she invested a good chunk of it in a creative planner company."

I furrowed my brow. "What in the world is a creative planner?"

"Honestly, I'm not really sure," Grandma said. "All I know is that there seems to be a lot of stickers and markers involved. It's amazing how many stationery supplies that girl has."

"Freya's always loved that sort of thing. She's very artistic," I said. "The complete opposite of me."

"You both have your strengths," Grandma said. "Freya is a very creative person, but she's not really business-minded. That's why this has me so worried."

"But surely Josh would have looked into it for her," I said. "He's good with finances. The butcher shop seems to be very successful."

"That's the problem. She didn't tell him how much money she put into it."

"She kept it a secret from her husband? Wow, that's not like her."

"Exactly. This whole thing has been out of character for her." Grandma paused while a couple of guys walked up to the diner. Once they were inside, she said, "She made me swear not to tell anyone about the financial pickle she's in, especially not Josh."

"But she can't keep it a secret forever."

"That's what I said." Grandma shook her head. "Freya told me she has a fool-proof plan to get her money back from her business partner. But I think it's highly unlikely that it will work."

"Who's her business partner?" I asked.

"Andrea Grimes." My grandmother spat the name out as though it left a nasty taste in her mouth.

My jaw dropped. “You’re kidding me. That woman is a real piece of work.”

Grandma held her hand up. “I know. That’s why I’m worried about your cousin. I’m afraid she’s going to do something stupid, and we all know what happened to the last person who crossed Andrea Grimes. She spread nasty rumors about him. The man ended up moving to another state.”

I ran my fingers through my hair, grimacing when I touched my bald spot. “There’s got to be something we can do.”

“Well, if anyone can figure out how to help, it’s you. You’re logical and level-headed. That’s the only reason I’m telling you about Freya’s situation.” My grandmother squeezed my hand. “Freya and Andrea are having a creative planner workshop at the library tomorrow morning. I think you should attend and, um . . .”

“Do some digging around?” I suggested.

“Exactly. There’s something fishy going on with this business. If you can figure out what it is, maybe we can get Freya out of this mess.” My grandmother pushed the door to the diner open, then glanced back at me. “By the way, what happened to your hair? It looks, um, different.”

“Maybe you should ask your friend, Hagrid, about that,” I said.

CHAPTER 2
GLITTERY PENS

The next morning, I went to the library for Freya's workshop. I was worried that I would be late—it had taken me ages to style my hair so that the bald spot didn't show—but I managed to get there with minutes to spare.

When I walked inside, my grandmother was helping a young mother check out a pile of picture books for her rambunctious toddler.

After she was finished, I asked, "Are you ever going to retire?"

"One of these days," Grandma said.

A dark-haired woman in her forties poked her head out from the back room. "What's this about you retiring, Rose? Who's going to take over as the library director?"

"This is how rumors get started. I don't have any plans to retire . . . yet." Grandma smiled at the woman, then turned to me. "I don't think you've met Wendy Chen before. She and her husband moved to Why a couple of years ago. They own an antique store, but Wendy still makes time to volunteer here several times a week. I don't know what we'd do without her."

"Word of advice," Wendy said to me. "Never run a business with your husband. Volunteering here is my form of escape."

Grandma looked at her watch. "Freya's workshop is about to start. The two of you better get going."

"Oh, I didn't know both of your granddaughters were into creative planning," Wendy said.

I held up my hand. "This is all new to me."

"Well, you're going to love it." Wendy grabbed a large tote bag from the back room, then we walked to the community room at the rear of the building. "I couldn't live without my planner. It's how I stay on top of everything. You know how it is."

Before I could reply, I heard my cousin's voice behind me. As I spun around, Freya squealed, "Thea, what are you doing here? When did you get into town?"

"Yesterday," I said as we embraced. "I decided to surprise everyone."

"I can't wait to catch up," she said. "But I have this workshop."

"I know. Grandma told me about it. I thought I'd

come, if that's okay."

"Of course." Freya tilted her head and gave me a mischievous grin. "But I never thought I'd see the day when Thea Olson would do anything even remotely crafty."

"Hey, I made those Christmas ornaments out of pine cones and sequins a couple of years ago."

"Uh-huh, and do you remember what happened with the glue gun?"

Wendy leaned forward. "What happened?"

"We made a pact to never talk about it," I said. "Right, Freya?"

"My lips are sealed," my cousin said. Then she stage whispered to Wendy, "I'll tell you later."

Freya's expression sobered as Andrea marched toward us.

"Why aren't you inside setting up the room?" Andrea scowled at my cousin. "We start in five minutes."

"I was waiting for you," Freya snapped. "You have the supplies, remember?"

Wendy looked uncomfortable. "Why don't we go grab some seats?" she suggested to me.

When we went inside, I was surprised to see such a meager turnout—only four other women besides Wendy and myself. Three of the women were sitting at a table near the front of the room. They waved at us in acknowledgment, then went back to chatting about their upcoming girls' trip to Las Vegas.

Jessica Moulton sat by herself at a neighboring table. Although only in her mid-twenties, she had already acquired a number of commercial properties throughout the town and surrounding area, including the historic building where Josh's butcher shop was located.

People admired Jessica's focus and drive—in just a few short years, she had become a self-made millionaire. But she wasn't well liked. When you live in a small town, being condescending and self-righteous doesn't get you very far. I was secretly relieved when Wendy steered me to another table so that I didn't have to make small talk with Jessica.

After a few minutes, Freya and Andrea walked into the room carrying several cardboard boxes.

"Are those the new sticker kits?" one of the women asked.

"They sure are. I can't wait for you to see them. They're super cute," Andrea said as she set her boxes down. Then she turned to my cousin. "Freya, open these up while I kick off the workshop."

Freya did not look thrilled at Andrea's dismissive tone, but she got to work unpacking the stationery supplies.

"Let's start with introductions." Andrea whipped a tiara out of her over-sized purse. She skillfully placed it on her head without mussing up a strand of her elaborate updo.

"For those who don't know me, I'm Andrea Grimes,

Prairie High prom queen of the class of—"

Fortunately, Gina Gianelli burst into the room, saving us from having to hear Andrea relive her high school glory days.

Gina and Andrea had been bitter rivals in high school, both vying to be captain of the cheerleading squad, prom queen, and class president, not to mention constantly fighting over guys.

The two women couldn't be more different. Gina was a large woman who had a fondness for blue eyeshadow, heavy eyeliner, and cat-themed clothing. Today she was sporting blue jeans and an oversized t-shirt which said, "I'm not single. I have a cat."

In contrast, Andrea was constantly dieting so that she could fit into her designer clothing. I had lost count of how many plastic surgery procedures she had undergone to try to hang onto her youth. I wish someone would tell her that the lip and cheek implants weren't having the desired effect.

"Sorry, I'm late," Gina said. "My car wouldn't start. I had to get Bobby Jorgenson to give me a ride."

Jessica sniffed. "I'm surprised Bobby hasn't had his car repossessed. The guy's always broke."

Gina ignored the younger woman's snide remark, instead saying to Freya, "We're getting free pens, right?"

"That's right," Freya said. "Everyone will get a limited edition pen from our new summer release."

"We'll do that later," Andrea said. "As I was saying,

my name is Andrea Grimes. I'm the founder and CEO of Perfectly Pretty Planners. And this is my assistant, Freya Schafer."

Freya pressed her lips together. "What Andrea meant to say was that I'm her business partner."

Andrea frowned at Freya, then turned to the group. "Today, we're going to learn how to layer stickers and washi tape to give our planners that extra pizazz. We'll be creating an adorable Fourth of July spread using samples from our latest release. You'll be able to purchase the complete kit at the end of the workshop. It comes with everything you need to do weekly spreads in your planner so that they're fun and functional."

When Freya deposited my supplies in front of me, I whispered, "What's washi tape?"

She chuckled. "It's decorative adhesive tape which comes in all sorts of different patterns. I know you're more of a plain tape kind of girl, but give it a chance."

Andrea clapped her hands. "Everyone ready? Okay, open your planners and let's get started." She seemed surprised that I didn't have a planner like the other ladies, then handed me some blank planner pages to work with.

The next two hours were excruciating. While I had to admit that the firecracker stickers were cute, I'm one of those people who keeps things simple. I didn't see how decorating your planner could make you more productive. Freya had to keep reminding me that things could be both creative and functional at the same time.

"Believe me, it's way more fun checking things off your to-do list if you use stickers and markers," Wendy told me.

At the end of the workshop, Andrea grabbed Jessica's planner. "Ladies, you have to see this."

Jessica tried to grab her planner back. "Hey, there's personal stuff in there."

"I just want to show everyone how you hand lettered the days of the week. The font you used is adorable." Andrea patted Jessica on the shoulder. "Don't worry, your secret is safe with me."

"What do you mean by that?" Jessica asked sharply.

"Just a joke, sweetie," Andrea said as she held Jessica's planner up in the air. A piece of paper fluttered out and landed in front of me on the table.

"Give me that." Jessica snatched the paper out of my hand. "That's private."

I wasn't sure what the big deal about an invoice was, but whatever.

Never missing a marketing opportunity, Andrea said to the group, "You know what Jessica needs, ladies? One of our clip-in planner pouches, so that she has a place to store loose papers."

Jessica arched an eyebrow. "Why don't you bring one by my office tonight? We can talk about planner accessories . . . and other things."

"Sure thing," Andrea said coolly. "Seven okay with you?"

Gina waved her hand in the air. "When do we get our pens?"

Andrea rolled her eyes. "Freya will hand them out."

"You're closer to the box they're in," Freya said.

"Fine, I'll do it." Andrea rummaged through the stationery supplies. "I don't see them."

"Let me look." Freya furrowed her brow as she searched the box. After a few moments, she pulled out a plastic bag. "Here they are, but there are only seven of them. The manufacturer must have made a mistake."

"You were responsible for the ordering," Andrea snapped.

"No, you were. Don't you remember when . . ." Freya's voice trailed off as she realized everyone was staring at the two of them. She gave us a forced smile. "Actually, it's worked out perfectly. There are seven attendees and there are seven pens."

Andrea narrowed her eyes as Freya passed the pens out. I wasn't sure what I was going to do with mine. The barrel was covered in green sparkles and there was a pink pineapple on the top of the pen cap. Not exactly my style.

Most of the other ladies were thrilled with their pens, talking about how smoothly the ink flowed and what a nice addition it would be to their collection.

The room went quiet when Andrea held up a set of stickers. "I thought you ladies might like a sneak peek at what we'll be releasing in the fall. These are part of our Fur Friends line. The color palette is really unique —all those lovely lime green, neon pink, and dark blue shades work beautifully together."

"Are those cats?" Gina squealed. She jumped out of her chair and rushed up to the front to get a better look at them. "I've gotta have those for my collection."

"Sorry, they won't be available until September," Freya told her.

"You know how much I love cats," Gina said. "Can't you give me the ones Andrea's holding?"

"Sorry, those are our one and only set," Freya said. "It's a sample from the manufacturer that I need to approve before they start production."

"I'll be the one doing the approval this time around. In fact, I need to remember to look at it tonight." Andrea made a show of placing the sticker sheet into a plastic sleeve that had "remember" printed on it in large black letters. As she tucked it in her oversized purse, she said to Gina, "I'm not sure you could afford them anyway. Disability checks can only stretch so far."

Gina lunged at Andrea. I thought the two of them were going to come to blows, but Freya pulled Gina away. As she escorted her out of the room, Gina called out, "You better watch your back, Andrea, because one of these days you're going to get your just desserts."

CHAPTER 3
STICKER BOOK DRAMA

“How did it go?” my grandmother asked me when I rejoined her at the circulation desk after the workshop.

“Well, I learned two important things,” I said. “Apparently, you can never have too many stickers and some people can’t let go of high school rivalries.”

Grandma chuckled. “Let me guess. Gina and Andrea were at it. There’s never been any love lost between those two.”

“That’s for sure,” I said. “Freya’s not too fond of Andrea either.”

“Did you get a chance to talk with her about what’s going on?” Grandma asked.

“No, she was too busy with the workshop. But we’re going to meet for coffee tomorrow.”

Wendy walked up to the desk with an enormous pile of stationery supplies in her arms. "They still have some sticker books available," she said to me. "You should grab some before they're sold out."

"I think I'll pass," I said. "I'm going to continue to keep track of things I have to do on my phone."

Wendy shrugged, then turned to my grandmother. "Want me to cover the desk for a while? I don't have to be back at the store for another hour."

"That would be great. It would give me a chance to catch up on the shelving." My grandmother pointed at a cart loaded with books. "Thea, why don't you grab that and help me?"

I groaned. "You're going to quiz me on the Dewey Decimal system again, aren't you?"

"Everybody in this family knows how to classify books by heart, even your grandfather." She wagged a finger at me. "You don't want to get rusty, do you?"

My grandmother grabbed a stack of graphic novels and went off to shelve them, leaving me in a secluded corner of the non-fiction section to work on the remaining items. While I was organizing books on the history of early settlers in North Dakota (they're classified under 978.4 in case you were wondering), I heard Freya and Andrea arguing in the next stack over.

There was a small gap in between the books on the shelves, enabling me to see the two of them. Andrea was standing with her arms folded across her chest while my cousin jabbed a finger in her direction. Part of me felt guilty about being so sneaky, but Freya was my favorite cousin and I needed to look out for her.

"We're partners," Freya said. "You need to treat me with the respect that I deserve." When Andrea didn't respond, she added, "Or at least treat my money with respect. If it hadn't been for my investment, the company would have been out of business by now."

"Your money is all that you're good for." Andrea snorted. "You don't know a thing about running a business. Like what happened when you tried to design a sticker book. What a disaster."

"Are you kidding me? The only reason that didn't work out was because of your incompetence."

Freya tried to walk away, but Andrea blocked her path. "No, you're not going anywhere. Not until we settle this once and for all. Because if we don't, I'm going to tell your husband—"

"Don't you dare threaten me." Freya glared at the other woman. "Gina was right. You should watch your back. You've made a lot of enemies in this town, including me."

Andrea let Freya pass this time, then stood there quietly for a few moments. After taking a few deep breaths, she walked out of the stacks.

I slumped against the bookshelf behind me and rubbed my temples. My cousin was usually a happy, bubbly person. I had never seen her like this before. It had almost seemed like she was threatening Andrea, but that couldn't have been what she was doing, could it? It was a good thing we were meeting for coffee tomorrow—Freya was caught in a bad situation. Hopefully, I could help before things got even worse.

* * *

The next morning, my grandmother made me my favorite breakfast—pannekaker. She served the light, eggy Norwegian pancakes with chokecherry jam that she and I had canned the previous year. After I ate my fill, Grandma asked me to run an errand for her.

"Do you mind going to the butcher shop? Josh set aside a roast for me," she said. "You haven't had a chance to see your brother yet, so I thought I'd make a nice dinner for all of us tonight."

I patted my stomach. "I feel like I've already gained five pounds since I've been here."

"Nonsense. It only looks like four at the most," she joked. "Now hurry up. I want to get the meat marinating."

When I walked into the butcher shop, I was surprised at how crowded it was, considering they had only opened a few minutes ago. It looked like Josh's business was booming. Which was good, considering Freya might have lost some of their savings investing in Andrea's business.

Josh smiled at me. "I heard you were back in town.

Here to pick up your grandma's order?"

"Uh-huh," I said, looking at the long line of customers.

"Do you mind grabbing it yourself?" he asked. "It's in the walk-in fridge in the back. Middle shelf on the left. It's marked Olson."

"No problem." As I walked through the swinging doors that led to the back room, I saw a steel door to my right. For some reason, a broom was jammed in the handle. I pulled it out and placed it back with the other brooms and mops in the corner. Then I pulled the door open. I pushed the plastic strip curtain in the entryway aside, and was immediately blasted with freezing cold air.

Glancing to the left, I noticed the shelves were covered in frost. Hadn't Josh said that the roast was in the fridge? This seemed more like the freezer. I started to turn around when something caught my eye. I stared at it in disbelief. Andrea Grimes was lying on the floor and from the looks of it, she was frozen to death.

CHAPTER 4
UFF DA

Intellectually, I knew Andrea was dead. But that didn't stop me from rushing over to try to help her. Eventually, I realized things were hopeless. I sat back on my heels and ran my fingers through my hair. How in the world did she end up in the freezer at the butcher shop?

After taking a few deep breaths, I pulled my phone out and dialed 911. The connection wasn't great, but I eventually got my point across. I was freezing, but I didn't feel right leaving Andrea's body unattended. As I watched over her, I noticed something odd. Andrea had always had a thick blond mane that she wore in elaborate dos. But now her scalp was covered with sparse, mousy brown hair. Had she been wearing a wig?

Looking around the freezer, I saw my answer—a blonde hair piece lying next to Andrea's purse. Although Andrea had treated my cousin horribly, I didn't want anyone to find her like this. She had been proud of her appearance. I walked over to pick up the wig, but it was frozen solid. That's when I noticed something sparkly lying next to it—one of the limited edition pineapple pens Freya had passed out at the workshop yesterday.

"Thea, are you okay back here?" I heard Josh call out. "The roast is in the fridge, not the freezer."

As he poked his head through the plastic strip curtain, I said, "I don't think you want to come in here."

Josh blanched when he saw Andrea's body. "What in the world . . ."

Hearing sirens in the distance, I said, "The police are on their way. Maybe you should go meet them out front."

I wrapped my arms around myself while I waited. Something niggled at me as I surveyed the scene, but I couldn't put my finger on it. Then I shook my head. My imagination was acting up. Probably a result of hypothermia setting in.

"In here?" a familiar man's voice said.

I rushed out and saw a paramedic and two police officers. The paramedic pushed past me and hustled inside the freezer. Maybe he could work a miracle and revive her, but I didn't think so.

The older police officer nodded at me, then began questioning Josh.

"It's great to see you, Sis," the younger police officer said to me. "But I wish it was under different circumstances."

As my brother pulled me into a bear hug, I broke down. "I'm getting snot all over your uniform, Leif," I said as I wiped tears away from my eyes.

"Shush, don't worry about that. It's polyester. Grandma can get it out easy."

"You're twenty-six years old." As I poked Leif in the chest, I was reminded about how much we looked like each other—hair so blond it was almost white, pale blue eyes like Grandpa, and a lanky build like Grandma. "Don't you think it's about time you started doing your own wash?"

Teasing my younger brother helped restore some sense of normalcy. Unfortunately, that only lasted until they wheeled Andrea's body out of the freezer.

"Thea's freezing," Leif said to Josh. "Do you have a coat or something around here?"

Josh put a quilted hunting jacket around my shoulders. "I'll get you some coffee."

The older officer pulled Leif aside. They spoke in hushed voices for a few minutes. When Josh came back with a steaming mug of coffee for me, Leif suggested that the three of us go outside while the other officer examined the scene.

We walked out the back door and sat at a picnic

table Josh used for lunch breaks during warmer weather.

"That's odd," Leif said as he looked back at the building.

"What's that?" I asked.

"That window next to the back door is broken," Leif said.

Josh twisted his body to see what Leif was pointing at. "Son of a gun. That darn Bobby Jorgenson."

"You think Bobby did that?" Leif asked.

Josh frowned. "You betcha. He wanted me to give him some steak last week for free. I know that guy's hard up, but I still have a business to run."

"You really should get some security cameras out here," Leif said. "Without evidence, it's going to be hard to prove that it was Bobby."

"When I signed the lease on this place, Jessica said she was going to install some for the entire building, but she never got around to it." Josh sighed. "Guess I'll have to do it myself."

Leif nodded, then pulled out a notebook. "I need to ask you guys some questions about what happened. Let's start with you, Josh. How did Andrea get into the freezer?"

"Heck, if I know," Josh said. "I got an order of shrimp in at closing time yesterday. She wasn't in there when I put it in the freezer."

"You didn't check the freezer when you got in this morning?" Leif asked.

Josh shook his head. "Nope. I was running a sale on brats. Customers were lining up out the door."

I sipped on my coffee while Leif continued to ask Josh a series of routine questions. Then I leaned forward. "What I don't understand is how she got locked in there."

"It doesn't make sense to me either," Josh said. "There's a safety release handle on the inside."

"Maybe she slipped on something, hit her head, and was knocked unconscious," Leif suggested. "Then she froze to death before she came to."

"No, it wasn't that," I said slowly. "I don't think it was an accident."

Leif furrowed his brow. "What do you mean?"

"There was a broom jammed into the handle. Even if Andrea had tried to get out, she wouldn't have been able to." I took a deep breath. "I think she may have been murdered."

* * *

After my announcement that I thought Andrea had been murdered, the rest of the day went from bad to worse. The police chief arrived on the scene and gave Leif a dressing down.

"Don't you look cozy, relaxing outside with your family," Chief Grumpy MacLeish said to my brother.

By the way, the chief's first name really isn't "Grumpy," but that's what folks in town called him behind his back. Everyone was counting down the days until he retired. Unfortunately, the man was only in his mid-fifties, so we had a while to wait.

"But I'm not—" Leif started to say.

The chief narrowed his eyes. "You should have hauled these two down to the station for questioning, not sat around chit-chatting over coffee."

"I'm the only one drinking coffee," I pointed out, which in hindsight probably wasn't helpful.

"Escort Miss Olson and Mr. Schafer to the station and take their statements," he said to the other officer at the scene.

"Thea has some important information that I think you should hear first," Leif said.

The chief pointed at my brother. "Go man the vehicle momentum enforcement post."

I rolled my eyes. Why not call it what it was—a speed trap.

Josh and I spent the next several hours at the police station answering endless questions about Andrea. At least they kept the coffee coming. Josh managed to speak with Freya and break the news to her about her business partner. He said that she was distraught. I wondered if she was upset because Andrea had been murdered or because she was worried that she might not get her investment back now.

Once we were finally allowed to leave, I went back to my grandparents' house. We had a quiet dinner (the roast Grandma originally planned was long forgotten), watched a Minnesota Twins game, then went to bed early.

The next morning, as we were sitting down to breakfast, Leif came bursting through the door. He ran his fingers through his hair while he paced back and forth.

Grandpa looked up from his feed supply catalog and frowned.

"Sit down before you wear a hole through that linoleum," Grandma said to Leif. She poured him a cup of coffee, then asked, "Now, what's got you so upset?"

"I've been taken off the murder investigation case," Leif said.

"Why?" I asked.

"Because . . ." Leif paused, then looked at our grandmother. "You better sit down."

Her brow creased as she sat on one of the oak chairs. "What's going on?"

"It's Freya. Someone called in an anonymous tip, and now she's the number one suspect."

Grandma gasped, then grabbed my grandfather's arm. Grandpa patted her hand, then turned to Leif. "Freya didn't do it," he said simply.

"Of course she didn't," Leif said. "But try telling the chief that. It's only a matter of time before he arrests Freya. She doesn't have an alibi for when the murder happened."

"Uff da," Grandma said, using a Norwegian phrase to express her dismay. "You can't let this happen."

Leif groaned. "I don't know what I can do. The chief has me on permanent speed trap duty."

"What exactly did this anonymous tipster say?" I asked my brother.

"Freya was seen going into the butcher shop the night Andrea was killed," Leif explained. "When Andrea was locked in the freezer, she tried to send a text message for help, but it didn't go through."

"I had a weak signal when I called 911," I said. "And that was with the door open."

"Exactly," Leif said. "With the door shut, she didn't have a chance of reaching anyone. But once her phone was taken out of the freezer and the battery recharged, the text was sent and we now know the approximate time she was locked in the freezer—a little before eight."

As Grandma refilled our coffee cups, she said, "It's perfectly natural that Freya would go there. It's her husband's shop, after all."

"But why go after hours?" I asked, playing devil's advocate.

Grandma shrugged. "Maybe Josh forgot to bring home some pork chops for dinner."

"Maybe." I turned to Leif. "Have they questioned Freya yet? What did she say?"

"They brought her in early this morning. From what I understand, she denied being anywhere near the butcher shop. She did admit to going for a drive last night around the time Andrea was killed. Apparently, she clammed up after that and demanded a lawyer." Leif took a sip of his coffee. "Josh is getting an attorney for her. In the meantime, I'm not supposed to be anywhere near the case because it involves family."

"I hate to admit it, but Chief Grumpy has a point," I said.

"Humph." Grandma pursed her lips. "I guess that means we'll have to help Freya in an unofficial capacity."

Leif's jaw dropped. "Please tell me you're not serious."

"I'm always serious, especially when it comes to my grandchildren," Grandma said sternly. "All we have to do is figure out who did it. Then that will be the end of it. And we need to do it before the Fourth of July. It's Freya's favorite holiday and we don't want her to miss the fireworks, do we?"

A slight smile played across Grandpa's face, then he got up from the table. "Think I'll head down to Swede's."

"Good idea," Grandma said to him. "See what gossip you overhear. Maybe someone will say something that will prove Freya's innocence."

After he left, Grandma leaned forward. "Okay, where do we start?"

"Hang on a minute." I dashed up to my room, then

came back down, waving a sparkly green pen in the air. "This is a limited edition pen, the same pen that was found next to Andrea's body."

"Where did you get it?" Grandma asked.

"At the workshop yesterday. There are only seven of them, including mine," I said.

"Well, we know you didn't kill Andrea," Leif said. "So that narrows the suspects down to six people."

"Actually, I think we can narrow it down even further. Three of the ladies there were heading to Vegas right after the workshop. If we can confirm that they did, in fact, go on their girls' trip, then that rules them out."

Leif nodded. "I'll have a quiet word with one of my buddies on the force."

"So who does that leave us?" Grandma asked.

"Wendy, Jessica, and Gina," I said.

Grandma sniffed. "It wasn't Wendy. She volunteers at the library."

Leif smiled. "I'm sure there are some serial killers who are voracious readers."

"I have to agree with Grandma. Wendy doesn't seem like a murderer," I said. "My money's on Gina. She got into it with Andrea yesterday."

"Gina does have a record," Leif said.

"Really? What for?" I asked.

"Shoplifting and disturbing the peace," he said. "Did you know she actually tried to steal some ground beef last month from Josh? He reported her and she's had a grudge against him ever since."

"Didn't you tell me that Gina threatened Andrea?" Grandma asked. "Something about 'Andrea getting her just desserts'?"

I gulped, knowing that I had overheard Freya saying something similar to Andrea while they were arguing in the stacks. But Freya was innocent. One of the other women wasn't. All we needed to do was prove it. I just wasn't sure how.

As if reading my thoughts, Grandma said to me, "Why don't you start with Jessica? She's usually at the laundromat at this time of day collecting money from the machines. See if you can find out what she was doing last night. If we can rule her out, then we know it was Gina for sure."

"I'm not sure this is a good idea," Leif said.

"It's the best idea we have," Grandma said to him. "Now, you help me clear the table while Thea pays Jessica a little visit."

CHAPTER 5
CANADIAN QUARTERS

I snatched a piece of bacon before my grandmother shooed me out of the house. Leif walked me to my car, carrying a basket of old towels that I was supposed to use as a pretext for visiting the laundromat.

"I still think this is a bad idea," Leif said. "Jessica will flip if she thinks you're sticking your nose in her business."

"Ah, but you're forgetting one important thing about Jessica—she loves to point out what everyone else is doing wrong. All I have to do is ask her if she thinks Chief MacLeish is up to the job of investigating a murder, then let the conversation go from there."

Leif chuckled. "You make police work sound so easy."

"Are you still glad you became a cop?" I asked him.

"For the most part. The chief can be a challenge to work for, but I like knowing I'm making a difference in our community." Leif cocked his head to one side. "How about you? How's your job going?"

"Gosh, look at the time." I grabbed the towels from Leif and shoved them in the back of my car. "I better get going."

I slipped into the front seat, but before I could close the car door, Leif said, "Not so fast, Sis. Tell me what's wrong."

"Later," I said. "We need to focus on Freya now. My problems are trivial in comparison."

As I drove into town, all I could think about was why I had run away from Minneapolis. Eventually, I was going to have to tell my family what had happened, but now was not the time. Clearing Freya's name was the priority.

The laundromat was located in a small strip mall that also housed a pizzeria and a taxidermist. It was convenient for people who wanted to do some wash, grab some lunch, and get a hunting trophy mounted all in the same afternoon.

As I walked inside the Sudsy Shack, the smell of laundry detergent and the whirring sound of the machines greeted me. Jessica was wrestling with the coin slot on a washer.

"Bulldog, how many times have I told you not to put Canadian quarters in here?" she snapped at an older man standing next to her.

"I didn't know they were Canadian," Bulldog mumbled.

She grunted as she yanked the coin slot. Once it was free, she shoved the offending coin in his face. "See this here? That's Queen Elizabeth. Last time I checked, we had a little thing called the American Revolution. We overthrew the monarch."

The older man peered at the quarter. "She seems like a nice lady."

Jessica pointed at the door. "You're banned. Get out of here."

"But the machines at the trailer court are busted. How am I supposed to do my wash?" Bulldog looked genuinely perplexed.

"Not my problem." Jessica put her hands on her hips, watching as he slunk out the door. After he left, she spun around and noticed me. "Thea, what are you doing here?"

I held up the basket of towels. "The washer at my grandparents' isn't working."

"Okay, just make sure you use American quarters."

I set my laundry basket on top of one of the machines, then walked over to the small office where Jessica was sorting coins. "Did you hear about Andrea?" I asked, poking my head through the door.

"Of course, it's all anyone can talk about," Jessica said without looking up.

"Did you know I found Andrea?"

Jessica sat back in her chair and gave me an

appraising look. "Really?"

"It was awful." A shiver passed through me as I recalled the events of yesterday. Sitting down in a plastic chair, I said, "I don't know what was worse, finding the poor woman or watching the chief blunder around the crime scene."

"That man is completely incompetent," she said. "Remember when there was that string of break-ins last year?"

"I heard about it. A number of your businesses were targeted, weren't they?"

She nodded. "It was obviously Bobby Jorgenson. His wallet was on the floor next to the cash register at my dry cleaners."

"What happened?"

"Bobby told the chief that he must have dropped it during business hours." She sniffed. "As if Bobby Jorgenson ever owned anything that needed to be dry cleaned. The chief said the evidence was 'inconclusive,'" Jessica said, making angry air quotes, "Bobby got off scot-free."

"I'm worried he's going to mess this case up, too." I leaned forward. "I think he's going to try to pin it on Freya."

"Why Freya?" Jessica asked as she fiddled with the coins on her desk.

"The chief thinks the person who did it was at the workshop yesterday." That was a fib. Chief Grumpy had his sights set on Freya and refused to consider any of the other workshop participants.

Jessica shifted in her chair. “That’s ridiculous.”

“Oh, I know that, but you know how the chief is. Once he gets fixated on an idea, there’s no letting go.” I paused, not sure how to direct the conversation the way I wanted it to go. Leif was right—investigating a crime was harder than it seemed. Finally, I decided to just go for it. “I assume the chief asked you for your alibi last night.”

“My alibi? Don’t you sound all official.” Jessica looked bemused. “But if you must know, it was bingo night. You’ll find me there every Tuesday night. Just ask Pastor Rob.”

“You play bingo?” I stifled a laugh. The thought of Jessica sitting in the church basement each week with multiple cards and a dauber in front of her was comical.

“Sure, you’d be surprised how big the jackpots get sometimes.”

Now it made sense. It was all about the money for her. I had what I'd come for—confirming that the woman had an alibi—so I stood and started to say goodbye. But Jessica cut me off.

“If the chief really thinks it was someone who was at the workshop, then he should be investigating Gina. After that business with Teddy Mann, I wouldn’t be surprised if she snapped.” When I gave her a questioning look, she added, “Teddy moved here six months ago—he’s in the oil business. Gina was practically drooling over him. He was nice to her, but she read more into it than there was."

Jessica paused to take a sip of her diet soda. "Gina was livid when she found out Teddy and Andrea were dating. Maybe that was the last straw."

"You think Gina killed Andrea because she was jealous?"

"Good enough reason as any." After a beat, Jessica asked with a mocking tone in her voice, "Do you have any more questions?"

"Actually, I do have one," I said. "I was surprised to see you at the workshop. You don't strike me as the type of person who's into stickers and washi tape."

Jessica rolled her eyes. "Oh, believe me, I'm not. Andrea begged me to come and I couldn't say no. At least now that she's gone, I won't have to do what she —" She cut herself off mid-sentence, then stood. "I better go check on the dryers. They've been acting up."

As she ushered me out of the office, I was left wondering what Andrea wanted Jessica to do. Then I shrugged. What did it matter now, anyway? I grabbed my basket of unwashed towels and got in the car. It was time to pay Gina a little visit.

* * *

The Enchanted Forest Trailer Park was on the outskirts of town, near the railroad. I'm not sure what the original owners were thinking when they named the place. There wasn't a tree in sight, just endless fields of sunflowers, and there was nothing even remotely enchanting about the place.

As I drove up to the office, a pack of mangy dogs chased after my vehicle. When I opened the car door, they growled at me, telling me that this was their territory. Little did they know that I had recently gone head-to-head with a buffalo. Literally head-to-head when Hagrid or Ferdinand or whatever his name was ate my hair. So aggressive dogs? Please. I wasn't worried about them.

I stepped out of the car, squared my shoulders, and growled back at them. One of them rolled on his back in submission while the others ran away. Since things weren't going so well for me on the job front back in Minneapolis, I considered exploring dog training as an alternative career path.

"Hey, weren't you at the laundromat earlier?"

I turned and saw Bulldog sitting on the stoop of the office door. He was holding a can of beer, despite the fact that it was only ten in the morning.

"You didn't bring my laundry back with you by any chance?" he asked. "That lady ran me off before I had a chance to grab it."

"Sorry."

"That's a real shame. I'm out of clean underwear." He downed the rest of his beer, then tossed the can on the ground. "What about beer? You don't happen to have a six-pack in that fancy car of yours? It's awful hot out here. A fellow could die of thirst."

"I hear water is very hydrating." Then I quickly changed the subject. "Do you know where the manager is?"

"You're looking at him." Bulldog belched, then gave me a toothy grin. "What can I do for you?"

"I was looking for Gina Gianelli. Can you tell me where her trailer is?"

"I can do better than that. I'll show you. Come on, Missy. Hop in." He got in the passenger seat of my car, then directed me to the far end of the park. He pointed at a dusty trailer on cinder blocks. "That's Gina's place."

"Thanks," I said, as I waited for him to get out of my car.

"Oh, don't mind me. I'll wait here while you go visit with Gina."

I was reluctant to leave Bulldog alone—he was already getting dirt all over the dashboard as he played with the radio controls—but I wasn't sure how to get him out of my car. I briefly considered growling at him like I had at the pack of dogs, but fortunately, Gina came to my rescue.

"Bulldog, get out of that lady's car," she bellowed through the screen door. The older man startled at the sound of her voice. Then he slunk out of the car. Gina watched him amble back toward the office for a moment, then turned to me. "What are you doing here, Thea?"

That's when I realized I didn't have a plan. I was standing in front of a potential killer. What was I supposed to do? Get her to confess to murder, then escort her to the police station?

When I didn't answer right away, Gina said, "I bet you're here to see my sticker collection. Come on in. I'll make us some coffee."

Gina put the kettle on while I took in my surroundings. Her trailer seemed smaller on the inside than the outside, probably because of the mountains of stuff piled everywhere. There were dozens of crocheted afghans, an enormous collection of stuffed animals, various knick-knacks, and tattered magazines strewn about. The dinette table was littered with stationery supplies. I also counted at least five cats—three napping in cardboard boxes, one nestled on top of the afghans, and another one batting washi tape off the table.

"Grab a seat," Gina said from the kitchenette. "Coffee will be ready in a jiff."

I pushed some old newspapers aside, then perched on the edge of the bench seat, which was covered in fur. "How long have you been collecting stickers?" I asked as she set a chipped mug in front of me.

"Oh, let's see, about three years." She scooped up some magazines from the seat opposite me, looked around for a moment as though perplexed that there wasn't any place to put them, then finally deposited them on the floor. "I use them in my cat planner."

"You have a planner for your cats?"

"Well, sure. How else would I know when it's feeding time?" She dug under a stack of mail and pulled out a colorful planner. Flipping it open to the current week, she said, "See how I put a cat sticker next to seven each morning and another one at five in the evening? That's when my babies get fed. I use different colors to signify their preferences—lime green means tuna, dark blue means chicken, and neon pink is for liver."

"If their feeding schedule is the same every day, can't you just remember that?" Realizing how rude that sounded, I quickly said, "Sorry, I'm new to planners. I don't really understand how they work."

"Don't worry, you'll get the hang of it," Gina said. "Word of warning, Andrea charges an arm and a leg for her sticker kits. There are cheaper places to get planner supplies. But her designs are so cute that sometimes I have a hard time resisting. I hope she runs an end-of-season sale so I can pick up some stuff."

I studied Gina. She seemed oblivious to the fact that Andrea was dead. But she was the killer, right? She had to have been the person who locked Andrea in the freezer. Jessica had an alibi and Wendy . . . could it have been Wendy?

While I mulled this over, Gina continued to chatter

on about stickers, washi tape, and pens. "You want to be careful which pens you use when you're writing on stickers. If the stickers have a shiny surface, a lot of pens will smudge."

She scrawled "catnip" on a heart-shaped sticker, then rubbed her finger across the writing. "See what I mean? It smeared."

"Hey, isn't that the pen we got at the workshop?" I asked.

"Uh-huh. It's cute, but it doesn't work on this type of stickers. I wish I had two of them—one for my collection and one to use."

"So if you still have your pen, that means that . . ." My voice trailed off as I realized Gina couldn't be the killer. If it wasn't Gina and it wasn't Jessica, that meant it had to have been Wendy. Grandma wasn't going to be pleased to learn that one of her volunteers had committed murder.

"That means what?" Gina prompted.

"Um, nothing. I was just thinking about Andrea." I cleared my throat. "I guess you haven't heard the news. She was murdered last night."

Gina nearly spit her coffee out before saying in a shrill voice, "Murder?" Then she slapped the table with her hand and cackled. "Good riddance."

"I know the two of you had your differences," I said.

"Oh, honey, you have no idea." Gina shook her head. "One thing's for sure, I'm not the only person in town who will be happy that she's gone."

The cat who was nestled in the afghans next to me yowled as if in agreement. Then he jumped onto the table and nudged my hand with his head.

"Wow, Tobias really likes you. He never comes up to strangers." Gina grabbed her phone. "Lean in. I want to take a picture of this."

While I scratched the cat's belly, Gina asked for my phone number, then texted me the picture. She was convinced that I'd want a copy so that I could remember this historic moment in Tobias' life. Eventually, Tobias decided he was tired of me, so I made my excuses and left. As I neared the trailer park office, my phone rang. When I pulled over to answer it, Bulldog tapped on my window.

"If you're heading back to the laundromat, would you mind doing a load of wash for me?" he asked plaintively. He shrugged when I held up my phone to show him I was on a call.

"Leif, I'm glad you called," I said. "Gina and Jessica couldn't have killed Andrea. That means that Wendy must have done it."

My brother was silent for a moment. "I hope you can prove it, and prove it fast," he said softly. "Because the chief just arrested Freya."

CHAPTER 6
A GIANT CAT WITH HORNS

After discussing how to break the news to our grandmother that there was a strong possibility that Wendy killed Andrea, Leif and I agreed to meet at Swede's during his lunch break to decide what to do next.

I snagged a spot near the diner and hopped out of my car. As I was grabbing my purse from the back seat, I heard a familiar grunting noise behind me. Having learned my lesson, I had ditched my strawberry-scented shampoo for one that smelled like coconut. You don't find many coconuts growing on trees in North Dakota, so hopefully, this buffalo hadn't developed a taste for them and, by extension, my hair.

When I turned around, I could swear that the buffalo's eyes lit up in recognition. He moved closer to me, then bowed his head.

"He wants you to scratch behind his ears," a passerby said.

The buffalo butted my arm gently with his head, like some sort of giant cat with horns.

Concerned that he might get more insistent with his headbutting and knock me to the ground, I said, "Fine, but only for a minute."

Leif walked down the sidewalk toward me, grinning as he caught sight of me stroking the buffalo. "I see you've met Twinkie."

"Twinkie? Let me guess, he likes cream-filled sponge cakes."

"Yep. I made the mistake of eating one in front of him."

"If I stick around much longer, I'm going to need a list of what foods to avoid." I rolled my eyes, then asked, "Why does everyone in this town have a different name for him?"

"No one can agree what to call him." Leif shrugged. "Guess we'll need to wait until he tells us what his real name is."

"When the animals start talking to you, you know you're in trouble." I gave the buffalo one last scratch, then Leif and I went inside the diner.

As Norma set water glasses down in front of us, she told me people were speculating about why I was back in town. “It’s because of a guy, isn’t it?” she asked.

“I thought it would be nice to visit my family, that’s all,” I said.

“You were right,” Norma shouted at two women seated in a booth. “Thea’s having troubles with her fellow.”

“Thea’s such a pretty girl,” one of the women said to her friend. “I wonder why her boyfriend broke up with her.”

Her friend said, “Do you think it’s because she wanted to get married and he didn’t?”

I threw my hands up in the air. “I don’t have a boyfriend.”

“It’s his loss.” Norma patted my shoulder.

“Seriously, no one broke up with me. There’s no boyfriend,” I said, addressing the room. “I can’t even remember the last time I was on a date.”

“I should fix her up with my nephew,” someone said. “He’s a dentist. Thea has that gap between her two front teeth. Maybe he could do something about that.”

I ran my fingers through my hair, cringing when I touched my bald spot, then blurted out, “If you really want to know what happened, well, a man I trusted betrayed me. I was fired because of him. I should have stayed back in Minneapolis and fought for my job, but I didn’t. Instead, I came back to Why to get away from all of it. Okay? Happy now?”

Everyone in the diner was dumbstruck for a few

moments, then they all started chatting to each other.

"Poor thing, her boyfriend betrayed her."

"Once a cheater, always a cheater. She's better off without him."

"My nephew also does teeth whitening. I should give him Thea's number."

I put my head in my hands and groaned. This isn't exactly how I planned on telling my family what had happened. Leif wisely said nothing. He just squeezed my hand, then asked Norma to bring us two chicken salad sandwiches and some coffee.

We ate in silence, then I pushed my plate to the side. "What are we going to do about Freya?" I lowered my voice so that nosy Norma wouldn't overhear.

"I wish the chief hadn't stuck me on speed trap duty." Leif rubbed his jaw. "I feel like there isn't anything I can do to help."

"Has your buddy filled you in on the investigation?" I asked.

"Yeah. I spoke to him after I hung up with you." Leif leaned forward. "It's not looking good for Freya. My buddy said that the chief decided to cover his bases and check out the other women who were at the workshop. Three of the ladies were in Vegas, and the others have alibis."

"Even Wendy?"

"She was at home with her husband all night." Leif motioned for refills.

After Norma had topped up our cups, I asked, "What was Gina's alibi?"

"Bulldog Wheedler."

"The manager at the trailer park? You're kidding."

"Nope. Bulldog got drunk Tuesday night and started shooting off his shotgun. Gina called 911 to report it."

"Well, I guess a police report is a pretty strong alibi." I sipped my coffee while I pondered this. "Either Wendy or Jessica must be lying about where they were that night. We just need to find out which one."

Leif shook his head. "If the chief thinks I'm even as much as sniffing around the investigation, he'll have my hide."

"I'll talk to them," I suggested.

"What are you going to do? Confronting a killer is dangerous."

"Don't worry. I have a plan." I pulled my limited edition pen out of my purse and set it on the table. "We know the killer dropped her pen in the walk-in freezer. Gina has her pen, so either Wendy or Jessica are missing theirs. We find out which one that is, and we've found the guilty party."

Leif looked skeptical. "You're going to chit-chat about pens?"

"Uh-huh. Wendy is obsessed with stationery, so that'll be easy."

"And how are you going to tackle Jessica?" he asked.

"She's obsessed with money, right?" I looked at my pen for a moment, then grinned at Leif. "I have an idea."

"What's that?"

I flagged Norma down and asked for the check, then turned back to my brother. "I'll tell you if it works. In the meantime, I've got to skedaddle. It's time to pay Wendy a visit at the library."

***

When I walked into the library, my grandmother wagged a finger at me. "Why do I have to hear about what happened at work from the mail carrier?"

"I literally left Swede's ten minutes ago," I said. "How could you have found out about it already?"

"You know how the rumor mill works in Why," Grandma said. "And it doesn't help that Norma and the mail carrier are an item."

Wendy looked up from the books she was scanning into the system. "Your grandmother says you worked in HR. Any idea what you're going to do next?"

Her question jolted me. I don't think I had fully processed the implications of losing my job until that very moment. I was unemployed. My stomach twisted in knots as I played the word "unemployed" over and over in my head.

I had been working steadily since I was fourteen years old. My first job had been at a pet store cleaning out cages. I held various other part-time jobs in high school and college, as well as helping on the family farm. When I graduated from college, I went straight into an entry-level job at a management consulting firm in Minneapolis. Over the next several years, I worked my way up the ranks, earning coveted promotions before hitting rock bottom, otherwise known as unemployment.

"Thea is an organizational development consultant," I heard my grandmother explain to Wendy. "She helps companies improve their performance."

Wendy's eyes lit up. "The pizza place could use your help. It's really gone downhill in the past year."

"That's true. When they're not skimping on the pepperoni, they're burning your pizza. But I don't really think that's something Thea can help with." Grandma gave me a gentle smile. "I'm sure you'll land on your feet."

"Why don't you hang up your own shingle?" Wendy asked. "I can't tell you how freeing it was when Mike and I started our antique business. Being your own boss is fabulous."

"I can imagine," I said, thinking about my former manager. The one who fired me without hearing my side of the story. The one who didn't bat an eye when someone else stole my work and presented it to a client as their own. Yep, being my own boss did sound appealing.

"You should go for it." Wendy reached into her tote bag and pulled out her planner. "I have a list in here of the people we used to set up our business."

As she flipped through her planner, I marveled at all the hand drawn doodles and intricate lettering she used on her pages. Was it really possible that adding creative touches to your planner helped increase your productivity? Maybe that was something I should suggest at my next client meeting . . . Oh, wait, unemployed people don't have client meetings.

"Where did it go? Oh, here it is. This is the name of our lawyer, the real estate agent, the accountant . . . oh, hang on, you definitely don't want to use that accountant."

"Who's that?" my grandmother asked.

"Booker Gillis. Andrea recommended him. Big mistake." Wendy pursed her lips. "He plays fast and loose with the rules. My husband and I were worried we'd end up in hot water with the IRS."

"He used to work in the Twin Cities for one of those big accounting firms, didn't he?" my grandmother asked.

"I think he got fired," Wendy said. Then she looked at me and her face reddened. "Sorry."

"It's okay." I shrugged, trying to pretend like it didn't bother me.

"Let me write the name of our new accountant

down," she said.

"Hey, is that the pen we got at the workshop?" I asked.

"Uh-huh," Wendy said. "I love gel pens, don't you?"

As she handed me the piece of paper with the contact details, a stocky man stormed up to the circulation desk. He slammed a large padded envelope down and glared at Wendy.

Wendy blanched. "Mike, what are you doing here?"

"We talked about this, Wendy," he said. "You promised you were going to stop buying stationery. We're supposed to be paying off our credit card debt, not adding to it. How many pens does one person need?"

"This is addressed to me. You had no business opening it." As Wendy grabbed the envelope, the contents went flying everywhere.

Grandma and I picked up washi tape, stickers, pens, and sequined paper clips off the floor while Wendy and her husband continued to argue. We replaced the items back into the envelope, then my grandmother politely suggested the couple take their discussion elsewhere.

After they left, Grandma shook her head. "Libraries are supposed to be sanctuaries, not a place to air your dirty laundry."

She grumbled for a few more minutes about the importance of indoor voices, then some middle school students asked for help with the computer stations.

While I waited for my grandmother to help the kids with their access codes, I breathed a sigh of relief. Wendy still had her limited edition pen. That meant she couldn't have killed Andrea. My grandmother would be pleased about that.

I was pleased too. By process of elimination, I now knew that Jessica was our killer. After sending a text to Leif with an update, I wandered over to look at the new releases. I had been so busy with work that I hadn't had much time to read. A book of whimsical cat illustrations caught my eye. Definitely right up Gina's alley.

As I perused the other books on display, something niggled at the back of my mind, but I couldn't put my finger on it. Did you ever get that feeling that something is staring you straight in the face, but you just can't see it? I was so sure that this investigation was cut and dry, but what if I was wrong?

CHAPTER 7
BINGO!

While I mulled over the investigation, I watched my grandmother bustle around the library, working her magic. Guided by her unwavering belief that reading nourishes our souls, she had an uncanny instinct when it came to matching patrons with books. So I wasn't surprised when she came back to the circulation desk and handed me a paperback.

My mind cast back to when my parents were killed in a car accident. Leif and I were just young kids at the time, struggling to understand that our mom and dad weren't coming back.

Our grandparents took us in, raising us as their own. I had found solace in reading. Somehow,

Grandma always knew what books would help me work through my grief. And here she was doing it again—presenting me with a collection of inspirational essays to comfort me as I dealt with the feelings of failure I was struggling with.

"Thanks," I said, giving her a kiss on the cheek. "I'll look forward to reading this later."

The last patron left, so I took advantage of the temporary lull to update my grandmother on the investigation.

"We can definitely rule Gina and Wendy out. They both have alibis—Wendy was with her husband at home, and Gina was at the trailer park when Bulldog Wheedler started shooting his gun off. I've also seen both of their pens."

Grandma frowned. "I don't feel comfortable that you were investigating Wendy."

"I know, but we had to look at all possibilities. The good news is that we're now one hundred percent sure she couldn't have done it."

"So that leaves Jessica," my grandmother said. "But you said she was at bingo that night."

"Maybe she was there for a while. She made sure Pastor Rob and other folks saw her, then slipped out to meet Andrea at the butcher shop." I looked off into the distance for a moment, then said, "It raises an interesting point though—why kill Andrea at the butcher's? Was it premeditated? Did she plan on locking Andrea in the freezer?"

My grandmother shushed me as an elderly man walked into the library. He waved at us, then settled down in a comfy armchair to read a magazine.

Grandma lowered her voice. "Jessica's office is in the same building as Josh's shop. Next door, in fact. What if Jessica made arrangements to meet Andrea at her office?"

"Actually, they did have a meeting scheduled for that night," I said, remembering the tense exchange the two women had at the workshop. "Andrea was going to show some planner supplies to Jessica. But I had a feeling there was more to the meeting than that."

"Perfect. We can place the two of them near the scene of the crime," my grandma said. "During their meeting, Jessica must have come up with some pretext for entering the butcher shop and asked Andrea to accompany her."

"You're good at this," I said, clapping my hands. "Jessica owns the building, so it's plausible that she has a key to the butcher shop. She probably shouldn't have one, but Josh is such a trusting guy. Maybe he gave her one, or he never changed the locks when he leased the space."

"I bet she told Andrea she smelled smoke." Grandma leaned forward, caught up in the excitement of solving the case. "Then she pushed Andrea in the freezer—"

"But Andrea fought back, and, in the process, her

wig fell off," I interjected.

My grandmother cocked her head to one side. "Andrea wore a wig?"

"Uh-huh. I was surprised to find out it wasn't her real hair. I think her wig was just one of many secrets that woman had." After a beat, I said, "Where were we? Oh, yeah. Jessica overpowered Andrea, slammed the door, and jammed it shut with a broom. Then she locked the back door and went back to bingo like nothing happened."

"Hmm." Grandma toyed with her scarf. "It all fits with what your grandfather heard at the diner this morning."

"With everything that's happened today, I forgot he was going to Swede's," I said. "Let me guess. Norma had some useful gossip."

"Actually, it wasn't Norma this time. Thor heard a couple of gals talking about bingo. One of the ladies was sitting next to Jessica on Tuesday. Jessica got bingo, but instead of jumping up and announcing it, she tucked the card in her purse and said that she had to go to the bathroom."

"Jessica passing up an opportunity to collect money? There's only one reason why she would do that," I said. "Because she had a meeting scheduled with Andrea at her office."

"Exactly." Grandma's eyes were sparkling. "They're having bingo again tonight—it's a special fundraiser for the food pantry. What do you say we go try our luck? We can ask around. Maybe someone saw Jessica leaving the church that night."

"If we can break Jessica's alibi and prove that she doesn't have her pen anymore, then the chief will be forced to admit that he was wrong about Freya." I rubbed my hands together. "I can't believe I'm saying this, but I'm actually looking forward to bingo."

* * *

I smiled when we pulled into the parking lot at St. Olaf's Lutheran church later that night. My grandfather was proud of our family's Norwegian heritage and made sure all his grandchildren knew Old Norse history. I always thought it was fitting that our church was named after one of the kings of Norway that I heard so many stories about growing up.

When we walked down into the church basement, my grandmother made a beeline for the kitchen, where several of her friends were setting out coffee and pastries. We had agreed that she'd talk to the regulars to see if anyone had seen Jessica leaving the church early during bingo. I was on a mission to find out if our suspect still had her pen.

Jessica was sitting at a table by herself, talking to someone on her phone. I slid into one of the empty seats next to her. Her back was turned to me and she seemed oblivious to my presence. Whoever was on the other end of the line, she certainly wasn't happy with them.

"How many times do I have to tell you?" Jessica sounded agitated. "The auditor is suspicious. He's given me ten days to come up with documentation that proves those purchases are legit."

She drummed her fingers on the table while the other person said something. Her body tensed, then she spat out, "You tell your associates that I'm putting an end to our little arrangement. You got that, Booker?"

Booker was an unusual name—it had to be that shady accountant Wendy had told me about.

As Jessica ended her call, I texted Leif.

See what you can find out about Booker Gillis. I think he might be connected to Andrea's murder.

When I looked up from my phone, Jessica was eying me warily. "I'm surprised to see you at bingo."

"My grandma persuaded me to come. Maybe I'll get lucky." I smiled at the other woman. "I seem to be on a hot streak lately. You know those limited edition pens we got at the workshop?"

"Those tacky things?" Jessica scoffed.

"Some people will pay a high price for tacky," I said. "In fact, I have a friend who offered to buy mine for a crazy amount of money. With Andrea's passing, they've become highly collectible."

Jessica looked intrigued. "How much money?"

I made up a number, and Jessica nearly jumped out

of her chair. "Do you think your friend will want to buy mine, too?"

"You still have yours?" I asked.

"Uh, sure. Tell you what, come by my office tomorrow afternoon and I'll show it to you."

"Sounds good," I said, not believing for a minute that she actually still had her pen. "I'm gonna grab some coffee before we get started. Want some?"

Jessica shook her head, and I scurried off to find my grandmother. I told her about Jessica's conversation with her accountant. "I think something fishy is going on with her finances. Maybe Andrea was in on it. Money is always a good motive for murder."

"I can do you one better." Grandma smiled. "One of my friends saw Jessica get into her car during bingo on Tuesday. She doesn't have an alibi."

Ginning back at her, I said, "I'm pretty sure she doesn't have a pen either. Case closed."

CHAPTER 8
THINGS DON'T GO TO PLAN

"I'll be right back. I think I left my phone on the table," I told my grandmother as we were walking through the church parking lot later that night. Bingo night had been a tremendous success. We had blown Jessica's alibi out of the water and she had even fallen for my story that the limited edition pen was worth a lot of money. And to top things off—I even won a few bucks.

After grabbing my phone, I decided to use the ladies' room before rejoining my grandmother. As I walked toward the restrooms, I heard a couple arguing in a small meeting room. It sounded like Wendy and her husband, Mike.

I should have turned around in order to give them some privacy. I'm embarrassed to admit this, but what

I did instead was stop and listen to their conversation. Was investigating Andrea's murder to blame? Had it turned me into a busybody?

In hindsight, I'm glad I eavesdropped because what sounded like an ordinary marital dispute at first ended up taking a worrying turn.

"You have to stop spending so much on stationery," Mike said. "We're barely getting by as it is."

"How is that my fault?" Wendy asked. "That huge bill from the IRS is your fault. You're the one who decided to hire Booker Gillis as our accountant."

"That's not true. We made that decision together."

"Hah. Like usual, you decided something unilaterally," Wendy said. "If it hadn't been for that tramp, Andrea, I might have been able to talk you out of it. But, no, all she had to do was bat her eyelashes at you while she recommended Booker. You couldn't hire him fast enough after that."

"Enough with your overactive imagination," Mike said.

"Oh, please, I saw you going into a seedy motel with Andrea. That wasn't my imagination," she scoffed.

"It was a business meeting," he snapped.

I bit back a laugh. Only a fool would buy that excuse, and Wendy was no fool. She continued to lay into him about his affair with Andrea.

Then Mike cut in. "Enough. She's dead. Let's leave

it in the past." When Wendy started to protest, he snapped, "Do you want me to go to the police and tell them I lied about the two of us being at home the night Andrea was killed? Because, if not, I don't want to hear another word out of you about this."

Wendy broke into tears. "I'm going home. Find yourself someplace else to sleep tonight."

Before she could spot me, I darted around the corner and hid next to a storage cabinet. After I was sure that both Wendy and Mike had left, I rejoined my grandmother in the parking lot.

She asked me what took me so long, and I mumbled an excuse about the paper towel dispenser jamming. My thoughts were a jumbled mess on the drive back to my grandparents' house. Should I tell my grandmother what I overheard? Did it matter that Wendy didn't have an alibi? I had seen her pen earlier in the day, so she couldn't have killed Andrea. But she had lied to the police and I needed to know why.

* * *

I ended up telling my grandmother about Wendy and Mike's fight later that night. Grandma was thoughtful as she sipped her chamomile tea. Eventually, she said, "I think we should focus on Jessica. I'm sure there's a logical explanation for why Wendy lied about her alibi."

She sounded sure of herself, but I could tell she was

troubled. And I was troubled too, tossing and turning throughout the night.

The next morning, I woke to the smell of bacon frying. When I went downstairs, Leif, Freya, and Josh were sitting at the kitchen table with plates of scrambled eggs, hash browns, and toast in front of them.

"Good morning, sleepyhead," Grandma said as she poured me a cup of coffee. "You missed your grandfather. He went to Williston to look at a tractor."

I nodded, then sat next to Freya. My cousin would normally never leave the house without doing her hair and makeup. But this morning, her hair was lanky, and she hadn't attempted to conceal the dark circles under her eyes. "How are you holding up?"

"Not great." Freya's eyes welled up. "Josh had to borrow money from his parents to pay my bail. Maybe it would have been better if I had stayed in jail."

Josh put his arm around her shoulders. "Hey, stop that. They were happy to help."

"The only reason you had to ask them was because I gave Andrea all the money we had been saving," Freya wailed. "When she told me I would triple my investment, I believed her. How could I have been so stupid?"

"You're not stupid," Josh said. "You're not the first person to be taken in by a con artist."

"Josh is right," I said. "Andrea took advantage of

your trusting nature."

Freya dabbed her eyes with a napkin. "I shouldn't have kept it a secret from Josh. I'll never forgive myself for that."

Grandma urged Freya to eat something, but she pushed her plate away.

"I'm not hungry. I'm going to go for a walk," Freya said. When Josh offered to accompany her, she shook her head, telling him she needed some time alone.

Once she left, the four of us talked about the meeting I had planned with Jessica in the afternoon.

"I don't want you going alone, Sis," Leif said. "If Jessica is the killer, and she feels like you're on to her, you could be her next victim."

"You're preaching to the choir." I held my hands up. "It'd be foolish to confront her on my own."

"I'm going with Thea," Grandma said.

Leif arched an eyebrow. "No offense, but I think we need someone there who is a little more intimidating."

Grandma frowned. "I can be intimidating. Just ask the kids who try to skateboard in the library."

"Actually, I was thinking more along the lines of Josh," Leif said.

"Count me in," Josh said. "My shop is right next door to Jessica's office, so it makes sense."

"Now remember that you're only there to verify that Jessica doesn't have her pen," Leif said to us.

"I think we should also confirm that she has a key

to the butcher shop," I said. "That would prove how she got in."

Leif nodded. "I guess that's okay. But Josh should ask about that. It'd be more natural coming from him."

"She could have broken the window by the back door and got in that way," Josh reminded us.

"I thought Bobby Jorgenson was the culprit," I said.

"Normally, he's the first person I think of when it comes to vandalism," Leif said. "But he was at the trailer park that night getting drunk and shooting off guns with his uncle, Bulldog Wheedler."

"That's right," I said. "Gina called the police to report them."

Leif gave a wry chuckle. "She didn't need to bother. You can set your clock based on Bulldog's drunken antics. He gets paid Tuesday afternoon and by Tuesday night he's drunk as all get out, shooting at rabbits and other critters."

"That man is a menace." Grandma shook her head. "One time, he came into the library with a cigarette. When I told him he wasn't allowed to smoke, do you know what he did? He opened up a book, put his cigarette inside the pages, then closed it. He thought it was the funniest thing."

"I hope you banned him," I said.

"Banned who?" Freya asked as she walked back into the kitchen.

"We were talking about Bulldog Wheedler," Josh explained.

"Didn't he serve time a while back?" Freya asked. "Maybe I should ask him for some pointers, considering I'll be spending the rest of my life behind bars."

As Josh tried to console his wife and convince her that we would prove her innocence, I felt a knot form in my stomach. What if we couldn't clear her name? What if Freya ended up being convicted of murder?

* * *

When I walked into the butcher shop later that afternoon, Josh was wrapping up some pork chops for a customer.

"Let me know how that new recipe turns out," Josh said to the woman. Then he turned to me. "Give me a sec."

While Josh gave his assistant instructions about how to use the meat grinder, I wandered into the back room. My eyes rested on the walk-in freezer. A chill went through me as I recalled how I had found Andrea's body inside. It was hard to believe that, in just a few minutes, we were going to have proof that Jessica was the murderer.

Josh walked into the back and hung up his apron. He clenched his fists, then took a deep breath and relaxed his hands. He gave me a brittle smile. "Let's do this."

"Hey, are you okay?" I asked.

"Why wouldn't I be okay?" He gave a slightly maniacal laugh and gestured at the freezer. "A woman was killed in there. Officials have been crawling all over the place. Obviously, I can't sell any of the meat stored back here. That'll cost a pretty penny to replace. Not that I have much left in the way of pennies because my wife gave all of our savings to that woman."

Josh paced around the room for a few moments before leaning against the wall. "Do you want to know what the worst thing about this is? Watching Freya blame herself. I've told her over and over that it's not her fault, but she won't listen to me."

"Give her time." I patted his arm, then said, "Maybe I should do this on my own."

"No way." Josh smoothed down his shirt. "I want to be there to watch Jessica squirm. Besides, Leif would have my head if he knew I let you go on your own."

"Okay," I said slowly. "But remember, this is just a casual conversation. We're not there to make her squirm, just to gather information. Got it?"

"You betcha," he said.

I became increasingly uneasy as we walked into Jessica's office. Josh did not look like a man who was there for a casual conversation. My suspicions were confirmed when he slammed his fist on Jessica's desk, knocking her laptop onto the floor.

"Admit it. You killed Andrea," he said in a low voice that sent shivers down my spine. "And you framed my wife for it."

Jessica's eyes widened. She wheeled her chair as far away from Josh as she could, then spluttered, "I didn't kill anyone."

I looked sharply at Josh, but the fight had gone out of him. His shoulders slumped as he sank into one of the visitor seats.

"What's going on here?" Jessica said to me. "I thought you were coming to see the pen, not bring your cousin's nut job of a husband with you to accuse me of murder."

"You have it?" I asked.

Jessica unlocked the top drawer of her desk and pulled the familiar sparkly green pineapple pen out. "It's right here." Before I could inspect it, she snatched it away. "Nope, no touching the goods until I see the money."

"Um, well . . . about that." I twisted my hands together, trying to figure out what to say next.

Josh cut to the chase. "Thea made the whole pen thing up. It's not public knowledge, but the killer left her pen at the scene."

"You were hoping I didn't have my pen, weren't you?" Jessica roared with laughter.

"Well, you were seen leaving the church during bingo," I said, throwing all caution to the wind. After Josh's outburst, it didn't seem like it mattered much.

"You don't have an alibi for when Andrea was killed."

That silenced the other woman. For probably the first time in her life, Jessica didn't seem sure of herself. "I want the two of you to leave," she sneered. Then she picked up her phone and dialed someone, probably her lawyer.

Josh and I walked back into the butcher's shop, both lost in our own thoughts. The shop was quiet, so Josh told his assistant he could head home early.

"I'm confused," Josh finally said to me. "Did Jessica do it or not?"

"Honestly, I'm confused too. Every one of our suspects has their pen."

Josh sighed. "I think I'm going to close up early."

"Good idea." I smiled. "Guess I'll do what I always do when I'm feeling a bit lost—go to the library."

CHAPTER 9
TIME FOR FIREWORKS!

Before going to the library, I stopped at Swede's to get a to-go coffee. Gina was in a booth by the window, opening up a package. When she saw me, her eyes lit up.

"Wait until you see what I got in the mail," she said. "Only a fellow stationery addict could understand."

"I'm not really that into stationery," I said.

"That's what you say now, but give it a couple of months. Before you know it, you'll be wanting all the things." Gina grinned as she showed me a stack of brightly colored scrapbook paper. "Isn't it gorgeous? A woman in Montana hand dyes each sheet."

Norma walked over and gave Gina a pointed look. "Are you going to order anything? These tables are for paying customers."

"I don't need to be treated like this." Gina shoved the paper back in the package, then flounced out of the diner.

"Better make sure your wallet is still in your purse," Norma said to me. "Gina might have walked off with it."

"I'm sure she wouldn't of . . ." My voice trailed off as I remembered Leif telling me about Gina's shoplifting record. Fortunately, my wallet was still in my purse, so I paid for my coffee and headed to the library.

My grandmother was relieved to see me. "Are you free for the rest of the afternoon?"

"Sure. I don't have anywhere else to be."

"Good, both my library assistants are out sick, and I don't have any volunteer help today."

"Wendy couldn't come in?" I asked.

"No, she's too busy packing." Grandma lowered her voice. "She's leaving her husband and moving back to Bismarck."

"I'm not surprised after hearing them argue last night." After a beat, I said cautiously, "I know you like Wendy, but she lied about her alibi."

"I agree it wasn't ideal, but I understand her reasoning. She suspected her husband and Andrea were having an affair. When she followed Mike to the motel that night, her suspicions were confirmed. Wendy confronted him, and they had a huge fight in the parking lot. The motel manager can attest to that."

My grandmother looked off into the distance. "Wendy was embarrassed. So when the police asked her where she was the night of Andrea's murder, she said she was at home with Mike. He went along with it."

"I guess he didn't want people to know about the affair either," I said. "Well, I'm glad to know that Wendy is innocent. Although, I am sorry about her marriage falling apart."

"Me too. Ironically, Andrea only went to the motel that night to end things with Mike. She was only there for a few minutes, then she left for her meeting with Jessica." Grandma looked off into the distance for a moment, then she pointed at a stack of books. "Mind shelving those?"

As I wandered over to the stacks, I paused in front of an oil painting of the woman who had founded Why's library back in the early 1900s. A woman who just happened to be my great-great-great grandmother. I think. I always get confused by how many "greats" it is. As I studied her face, I felt the strangest feeling—like she and the library were calling me back home.

Shaking off the fanciful thought, I got busy with my shelving duties. As I was organizing some books on cat breeds (classified under 636.8 according to Mr. Dewey), one of them fell and landed on my foot.

Wincing, I picked it up and placed it back on the shelf. It promptly fell down again, narrowly missing my head this time. I put it back in its place and it slid off the shelf again.

What was going on? Was there something wrong with the shelf? No, that couldn't be it. The other books weren't budging. I examined the book in my hand, but couldn't find any reason for it to not stay in place. The shelf was attached to the wall, so there was no way anyone could be pushing it out from behind.

Staring at the book in my hand, I wondered if I was going crazy. Then it hit me—I knew who had killed Andrea. I just needed to confirm two things. Then the police would be able to put the murderer behind bars.

I sent a text to Freya and Leif, telling them I had solved the case. When they asked for details, I told them to meet me at our grandparents' house that evening and I'd explain everything.

Tucking my phone back in my purse, I looked at the cat book in my hand. I wonder what will happen if I try to reshelve this? I asked myself. I put it back on the shelf, held my breath, and moved out of the way. Wouldn't you know it—the book stayed in its place. Almost as though its work was done.

* * *

"Are you sure this is going to work?" Freya asked me and Leif as she wrung her hands. "I don't know why we couldn't do this last night."

It was the next day and the three of us were sitting at a picnic table at the far end of the town square. The Fourth of July festivities were in full swing—kids were running around with sparklers, people were munching on hamburgers and hot dogs, and the high school band was playing John Philip Sousa's The Stars and Stripes Forever.

"Because Chief MacLeish wouldn't listen to me when I told him Thea's theory," Leif said. "The only way he'll be convinced that you didn't murder Andrea is if we can get the actual killer to confess."

I waved my hand at the crowd. "And if we get the confession in front of all these people, then the chief will have to admit that he was wrong."

Freya nodded. "Okay, let's get this over with."

After the band finished their performance, Freya walked up to the mayor and whispered something in his ear. He looked surprised, then he addressed the crowd. "Everyone, listen up. Freya Schafer has a special announcement to make."

He handed her the microphone. Freya cleared her throat, then said, "As you know, Andrea Grimes passed away this week. In her memory, I've decided to hold an impromptu contest. Andrea was passionate about creative planning. So, if you have your planner with you today, bring it up to the bandstand, show me your favorite stickers, and you'll be entered into a prize draw for stationery supplies."

I was surprised to see how many people rushed forward. Who knew there were so many planner fanatics in town and that they carried their planners with them everywhere? Leif and I stood next to Freya as she looked at planner after planner. When Gina got to the front of the line, I said to her, "I hope you brought your cat planner with you. I thought you did some really cute decorations in it."

"I never leave home without it. Here you go," she said as she handed it to me.

I flipped through the pages until I found the one I was looking for, then showed it to Freya. She stared at the lime green, neon pink, and dark blue stickers for a moment, then sat back in her chair.

"Those are them," she said quietly.

"I hope I win the prize. I could use some more washi tape," Gina said, oblivious to Freya's discomfort.

Leif angled himself next to Gina so that he was blocking her path.

"You stole these cat stickers when you murdered Andrea," I said loudly, displaying Gina's planner to the crowd.

Gina's eyes darted back and forth. "I don't know what you're talking about."

Freya pointed at Gina's planner. "Those are from the sample sheet that Andrea showed at the workshop. The one she put in her purse to take home."

"I saw them when I was at your trailer earlier this week," I said. "I didn't make the connection until later at the library. Then I remembered the picture you took of your cat, Tobias. Your cat planner with these very same stickers was visible in the photo. You had sent a copy of the picture to me, and I showed it to Freya. She was certain that those were the stickers that Andrea had in her possession, and, now seeing them in person, she's confirmed it."

The three women who had gone on the girls' trip to Vegas were standing nearby. "I remember those stickers from the workshop, too," one of them said.

Another one looked at Leif. "Is that why you called yesterday to ask about my pen?"

"That's right," he replied. "You thought you had lost yours, but I suspect Gina stole it during a break at the workshop."

Gina tried to elbow her way past Leif, but he stood solidly in her way. "I didn't steal anything, and I certainly didn't kill anyone," she said, jabbing him in the chest.

"How else do you explain the stickers?" I asked.

"But I have an alibi. I was at the trailer park that night." She smiled at Leif. "You can't pin anything on me. I filed a police report when Andrea was killed."

"Everyone knows that Bulldog Wheedler gets drunk on Tuesday nights. It's like clockwork. You could have been anywhere when you made that call," Leif said.

At this point, I noticed Chief MacLeish was standing off to the side, carefully observing what was going on.

One of the women who went to Vegas turned to the chief. "Well, are you going to stand around here all afternoon or are you going to take Gina in for questioning? I heard her threaten Andrea at the workshop, and now there's these stolen stickers and pen. Seems like you'd want to be looking into that."

Freya whispered to me, "That's the mayor's new wife. She doesn't get along with the chief."

"Well, um . . ." The chief seemed at a loss for words. Then he turned to Leif and barked, "Well, you heard the lady. Take Miss Gianelli in for questioning."

* * *

Leif made it back in time for the fireworks. As he found a spot on one of our family's picnic blankets, he told us that Gina had confessed to Andrea's murder.

Freya started sobbing in relief as Josh pulled her into his arms. Grandma grinned from ear-to-ear, Leif and I exchanged high fives, and, much to everyone's surprise, Grandpa let out a whoop.

"Are there any details you can share?" Josh asked Leif. "Why my shop?"

"I think that locking Andrea in your freezer was part opportunity and part payback," Leif said.

"Payback?" Josh shook his head. "She did it

because I reported her for stealing ground beef? That's kind of extreme."

"Yeah. She's been holding a grudge about that." Leif looked at Freya and me. "I'm not sure what happened at the workshop, but Gina finally flipped. She heard Andrea arranging to meet Jessica that night at her office."

"Which just happens to be next to the butcher shop," Grandma pointed out.

"Correct. Gina followed Andrea there." Leif turned to Freya. "That's when Gina saw you driving past the butcher shop."

"I was so upset about losing our savings that I went for a drive that night to think," Freya said as she squeezed Josh's hand.

Josh gave her a gentle smile, then said, "Does that mean Gina called the anonymous tip line later that night?"

Leif nodded. "Uh-huh. Part of her revenge against you was trying to pin the blame on Freya."

"What happened after Gina followed Andrea?" my grandmother asked.

"She waited outside the office while Andrea and Jessica met. Oh, by the way, the police have another case to investigate. Apparently, Andrea and Jessica have been committing financial fraud. They were in cahoots with their accountant, Booker Giles. Gina heard the two women talking about it through the window." Leif put his fingers to his lips. "Not that you heard it from me."

"Bet she told you that as leverage for a reduced sentence," I said.

"I'm not sure it will help." Leif leaned forward. "Want to hear the rest of the story?"

"Hurry up," Grandma said. "The fireworks are starting soon. It's Freya's favorite part of the Fourth of July."

Freya laughed. "I'd say I have a new favorite part—being cleared of murder."

Leif smiled at her, then turned back to Grandma. "Okay, here's the short version. When Andrea left Jessica's office, Gina followed her to the parking lot at the back of the building. She pulled a knife on Andrea. They went over to the back door of the butcher shop, then she had Andrea break the window."

"So that's how she got in," Josh said.

"That's right. I'm not sure she originally planned on killing Andrea, but when she saw your shop, she got the idea to lock her in the freezer. She thought it was the perfect end to the Ice Queen, as she called her."

"If only Gina hadn't stolen those cat stickers," I said. "She might have gotten away with it."

"I'm so grateful to all of you," Josh said, his voice cracking with emotion. "If you hadn't investigated, my wife could have been locked up for good."

We were all silent for a moment, then Grandpa said, "Fireworks are starting."

After the spectacular display was over, I helped my grandmother pack up.

"Did anything strange ever happen to you at the library?" I asked her tentatively.

"What do you mean, dear?"

I shook my head. "Never mind, it's silly."

"Try me," she said as she folded a blanket.

"Well, the only reason I remembered that I had seen those stickers when I visited Gina at her trailer was because a cat book kept falling off the shelf. Over and over, like it was trying to tell me something."

"Sounds like it was," my grandmother said simply.

I shook my head. "No, I'm sure there's a logical explanation for what happened."

"You know what I always say about libraries." My grandmother grabbed my hand. "If you come with an open mind and a curious heart, you'll find the answers you seek."

"I think the library wants me to come home," I said quietly. "Wendy was right. I could start my own consulting business. These days, you can do so much virtually and work from anywhere."

"The library is a wise place. Maybe you should listen to what it says."

I took a deep breath, then said, "I'm going to do it. I'm going to move back to Why."

"That makes me so happy." She chuckled. "Besides, with Wendy gone, we could use a new volunteer."

As my grandmother and I hugged, I heard a

familiar snorting behind me. I turned around and smiled at the buffalo. “I’m only staying on one condition,” I said to him. “You leave my hair alone.”

GRANDMA OLSON'S RECIPES

Grandma Olson loves to cook for her family and friends. Here are a couple of her favorite recipes.

Pannekaker

Pannekaker is Thea's favorite breakfast. She loves these eggy Norweigian pancakes served with homemade chokecherry jam.

Ingredients

- 1 cup all-purpose flour
- 2 teaspoons sugar
- ¼ teaspoon salt
- 3 eggs
- 1 ½ cups full fat milk
- 2 tablespoons melted butter, plus more for cooking

Directions

1. Whisk the flour, sugar, and salt together in a large bowl.
2. Mix the eggs, milk, and melted butter together in a separate bowl.
3. Make a well in the flour mixture. Add the egg mixture into the well and stir into the flour mixture until combined.
4. Let the batter rest for 20 minutes.
5. Heat a skillet over medium-low heat. Add a pat of butter. Once melted, pour in ¼ cup of batter. Twirl the pan until the bottom is coated with butter.
6. Cook until the top is set and you see a few bubbles (approximately 30-60 seconds).
7. Carefully slide a spatula under the pancake and flip over.
8. Cook until the other side is set and golden brown (approximately 30-60 seconds).
9. Repeat with the remaning batter.
10. Serve with your favorite toppings such as fresh blueberries, chokecherry jam, or powdered sugar.

Guilty as Sin Gelatin Salad

Grandma Olson is known for her gelatin salads. She serves them at family gatherings, community events, church suppers and the like. Her sense of humor shows through with this particular recipe. It only has one maraschino cherry in it, and Grandma Olson always says that whoever gets it in their serving is guilty of something. She often used this trick when Thea and Leif were growing up. If one of the kids had done something naughty and hadn't admitted to it, she'd serve this salad, making sure they got the cherry. Inevitably, the child would immediately confess.

Ingredients

- 6 oz package of lime gelatin
- 2 cups boiling water
- 1 cup cottage cheese
- 1 cup mayonnaise
- 1 ½ cups diced canned pineapple
- ½ cup chopped walnuts
- 1 maraschino cherry

Directions

1. Dissolve the gelatin in the boiling water. Allow to cool.
2. In a separate bowl, mix the cottage cheese and mayonnaise until smooth.
3. Combine the cottage cheese-mayonnaise mixture into the gelatin.
4. Stir in the pineapple and walnuts.
5. Add the maraschino cherry.
6. Grease an 8 cup mold with cooking spray.
7. Pour the gelatin mixture into the mold.

8. Cover and refrigerate until set.
9. Unmold the salad, placing it on a serving dish.
10. Whoever gets the cherry in their serving is guilty of something . . . maybe even murder.

AUTHOR'S NOTE

Thank you so much for reading my book! If you enjoyed it, I'd be grateful if you would consider leaving a short review on the site where you purchased it and/or on Goodreads. Reviews help other readers find my books while also encouraging me to keep writing.

I hope you enjoyed this prequel to my North Dakota Library Mysteries series. I was inspired to write this series by two important people in my life—my sister and my husband. My sister works in a library and is passionate about books and reading. My hubby is a proud born-and-bred North Dakotan who gets a kick out of the fact that I'm writing cozy mysteries set in his home state.

Like Freya and some of the other ladies in this novella, I'm a bit of a stationery addict. My husband can't understand why I need so many pens and is utterly perplexed by my love of washi tape and stickers. He was rather amused by the fact that I based an entire story around stationery. Who knows – maybe one day I'll write some more books featuring my love of all things planner and stationery related!

Find out more about me and my other books at ellenjacobsonauthor.com. For news about my latest releases, sign up for my newsletter at:
https://www.subscribepage.com/m4g9m4

ABOUT THE AUTHOR

Ellen Jacobson is a chocolate obsessed cat lover who writes cozy mysteries and romantic comedies. After working in Scotland and New Zealand for several years, she returned to the States, lived aboard a sailboat, traveled around in a tiny camper, and is now settled in a small town in northern Oregon with her husband and an imaginary cat named Simon.

Find out more at ellenjacobsonauthor.com

ALSO BY ELLEN JACOBSON

North Dakota Library Mysteries

Planning for Murder

Mollie McGhie Mysteries

Robbery at the Roller Derby
Murder at the Marina
Bodies in the Boatyard
Poisoned by the Pier
Buried by the Beach
Dead in the Dinghy
Shooting by the Sea
Overboard on the Ocean
Murder Aboard the Mistletoe

The Mollie McGhie Cozy Mystery Collection: Books 1-3
The Mollie McGhie Cozy Mystery Collection: Books 4-6

Smitten with Travel Romantic Comedies

Smitten with Ravioli
Smitten with Croissants
Smitten with Strudel
Smitten with Candy Canes

The Smitten with Travel Collection: Books 1-3

Made in the USA
Las Vegas, NV
22 March 2024